Sammy and Sally's Sunday

Om KIDZ
An imprint of Om Books International

Om Kidz | Om Books International

Reprinted in 2023

Corporate & Editorial Office
A-12, Sector 64, Noida 201 301
Uttar Pradesh, India
Phone: +91 120 477 4100
Email: editorial@ombooks.com
Website: www.ombooksinternational.com

Sales Office
107, Ansari Road, Darya Ganj
New Delhi 110 002, India
Phone: +91 11 4000 9000
Email: sales@ombooks.com
Website: www.ombooks.com

ISBN: 978-93-52760-34-3

Printed in India

10 9 8 7 6 5 4 3 2

Sammy and Sally's Sunday

Paste your photograph here

My name is

____

Sammy is a **sweet** little boy. He is **six** years old.

Sammy has a **sister.**

She is **seven** years old.

Her name is **Sally.**

Sally and **Sammy**

are **sleeping** now.

The **stars** too, have gone to **sleep.** **Soon** it is morning. It is a **sunny** **Sunday** morning. There is no **school** today.

Sammy and **Sally spring** out of bed and take a bath.

Sammy wears his favourite jacket and **Sally,** her new **skirt.** They wear **socks** and **squeaky** clean **shoes.**

Sam and **Sally's** father is taking them to buy **sweets.**

Sammy and **Sally squeal** with delight as they rush downstairs.

They **sing** all the way to the **shop.**
Sammy and **Sally** can **see** it
full of **sticky** yummy **sweets.**
But the **shop** is closed!

SWEET SHOP
CLOSE

Sammy and **Sally** feel **sad.**

Their father is **sorry** for them.

Sammy starts to **sob.**

Sally is **sniffing.**

Their father wants to do **something special** for them.

All of a **sudden,** he **sees** a **sign** across the **street.**

Sammy and **Sally's** father points across the **street.**

They **stop sobbing** and **sniffing.**

There's a magic **show** nearby.

Sammy and **Sally** are now **smiling.**

They walk across the **street.**

A man is **selling** tickets.

Their father buys **some** tickets.

Sammy and Sally are so excited.

The **silent stage** comes alive.

The magician waves a **silvery** cloth.

Sparkling stars appear.

Sammy and **Sally stare** in delight. **Suddenly** a **snow**-white pigeon pops out of the cloth. There are lots more magical **surprises**.

Sammy and **Sally** love the magic **show**. They **sing** happily on their way back. They are **sure** they want to become magicians when they grow up.

Know your words

Naming words

Sammy	Sunday	shoes	street
sister	school	sweets	stage
Sally	skirt	shop	seats
stars	socks	sign	songs

Describing words

sweet	sticky	silvery
six	sad	superb
seven	sorry	sparkling
squeaky	special	snow-white
squeal	silent	

Doing words

sleep	sob	selling
sleeping	sniffing	starts
sing	stop	sit
see	smiling	stare
says		

Sight words

she	soon	some
something	sudden	sure
surprises		

Colour the cupcakes with words beginning with 's'.

Spot 5 differences between the given pictures.

Match the following based on the story.

Skirt • • 

Jacket • • 

Sweets • • 

Ticket • •